The Holy Book of
Ma'Swamp
And the sacred texts of The Ogrelord

This is a work of fiction. All characters and events portrayed in this book either are products of the author's imagination or are used fictitiously.

THE HOLY BOOK OF MA'SWAMP

All rights reserved.

www.MaSwamp.com

Cover by Randall Emmons

Published by Past the Pine Publishing
1590 Brandyhill Drive
Rock Hill, South Carolina 29732

www.PastThePine.com

ISBN 978-0-9979143-9-9

First Edition - Copyright 2016

Printed in the United States of America

Written by Jacob Emmons

The Holy Book of
Ma'Swamp
And the sacred texts of The Ogrelord

To Chase and Spencer,

Yo thanks lil' dawgs. I hope you like this book you kiddos. Happy Halloween in November!

~ Lord Sabe

To my friends, for making me start a joke that took up eighty-seven pages, and not once attempting to stop me.

To my parents, for letting the joke get so out of hand that you helped me finish it.

And to Mrs. DiMatteo, who taught me to color mark, annotate, and dissect my own writings to make them better.

Chapter I: The Realms
Creation of the Three Realms:

There was Him, who was the One Beyond All, who in Far Far Away is called The Ogrelord. He made the world in His divinity. At first there was nothing, then He, The Ogrelord, looked upon the emptiness of the Void around him, and willed all of the realms into being. Far Far Away, the realm of Men, was the first.

He created this realm by taking the wax from His ear and setting it upon the Void, making the flat form of the realms.

Aeterna Flamma was the next realm, created from the grime underneath the Ogrelord's fantastical fingernails.

The last realm the Ogrelord created was Ma'Swamp, a realm for His avatar to reside in, made from the mold in between The Ogrelord's toes.

Each world has its own properties, problems, and they stay in solitude for a majority of the time. Each realm took form, and became a sentient entity. The entities govern all within themselves and are able to meet together to discuss events going on and the best ways to solve problems.

Making of The Realms' Creations:

The One Beyond All called to His realms, who are sentient entities, and asked them to create beings to populate the realms He created. They obliged, and with the gift He had given them, The Sacred Onions, the realms created beings in their own images to reside within their borders. He told them, "We know what we are, but not what we may be."

With those words of encouragement, the entities of the realms got to work. Far Far Away made Men, and in its own shape, Men were given two arms, two legs, a head, and a body. These Men were made fragile, but intellectual; able to outthink any foe that they could not battle. These soon grew to have Layer, a sacred divine tether to The Ogrelord.

Aeterna Flamma made beings in its own image, The Legionnaires, who are remarkable in battle, but not intelligent, and in the absence of intelligence and wit, Aeterna Flamma conceived a new thought and made another, more powerful being, the King Regent, who was a being of immense evil that quickly became the ruler of The Legionnaires, overtaking them easily with his wit. He commanded them with his nefarious cunning.

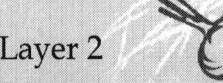

Ma'Swamp created but two beings, The Incarnation, the avatar of The Ogrelord, who had no idea of his true beginning, and Faye, his wife. The Ogrelord therefore became life.

The Ogrelord was ogrejoyed with these creations, and then shared His true gift with the three Realms, the All-Star. The All-Star was an item shared amongst the realms to help share the knowledge of the Ogrelord through all of the people. Many beings shied away from this gift, the Legionnaires most of all. Men slowly began to accept the All-Star, which gave them sight past the simple constructs around them.

It began to give them wisdom that only the Ogrelord had previously possessed. They then had more open knowledge of the existence of their great creator.

Many Men became corrupted by the All-Star, which had been made into a fountain in the center of Far Far Away. These wicked Men drank more than they should have from the Fountain all at once. The Fountain's power caused them to become something greater than what they could ever have been otherwise.

This created an entirely new breed of Men; and for their avarice, the Ogrelord changed them. He removed their names and their titles, then He renamed them and gave them new purpose.

Layer 3

The ones who grew hair, claws and teeth, He named the Three Bears, and moved them to the forest on the outskirts of the land between Far Far Away and the nearly impenetrable wall of Ma'Swamp. To the one who became wooden, He gave the title Pinocchio, and left him in the care of one kind old man in the forest. To the one who grew hooves, a longer face, and a tail, he named Dawwnkeh, and he placed Dawwnkeh on the gate to Ma'Swamp to protect it, and lead wanderers into Ma'Swamp.

Many more were created, and eventually so many were placed in the forest, that Men took to calling it the Enchanted Forest. It became the new home for many "Fairy Tale" creatures, many of whom were revered by Men. However, many were also feared, so Men left the Enchanted Forest to its own.

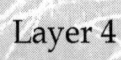

As the years went by, The Ogrelord came to notice that many of these Men were not finding each other to be suitable mates, and therefore would not reproduce. This shocked The Ogrelord, as He did not know why. He sat in Ma'Swamp, pondering the reason why they would not populate His realms, and therefore would go without having a child. He then thought of the answer to this problem: love. The Ogrelord would give all Men a piece of His divine entity, His Layer, and this layer would allow Men to feel love for one another, and reproduce with each other, fully aware of the long, costly consequences and the tough years ahead. They would stick with each other through thick and thin, and always care. The Ogrelord then became love.

The Ogrelord then became absent from the realms, and went off for many generations in order to let the realms govern themselves. The realm of Aeterna Flamma became twisted and corrupt, the current King Regent, King Regent IV, made his subjects build large monuments to honor him and many large, stone castles for him to live in while they lived in squalor.

They feared the awesome power that would come from a union of The Incarnation and Faye. The beings of Aeterna Flamma kidnapped Faye from the land past the border of Ma'Swamp. They wiped all memory of her existence from The Incarnation's mind when they attacked him. They dumped Faye across the border into Far Far Away. Since no ogres may fully exist in other realms, Faye was cursed to live as an ogre only at night, while during the day she existed a human. The Legionnaires took Faye to the realm of Far Far Away, where she became an infant due to reasons unknown.

In Far Far Away, a caring family took her in and raised her as their own. The Incarnation could not remember his mate, but knew in the back of his mind that he was missing her. Without her, he reverted to being a youth, forced to grow up all over again without his wife to help him. The Incarnation became very lonely, irritable, and grumpy. He lived all alone in his swamp.

Ma'Swamp:

Being the home of The Ogrelord, the Incarnation, and the souls of the deceased, Ma'Swamp was one of the most detailed creations of The Ogrelord. His influence over it still continues to modify and change its very structure and its surroundings.

There are many things to do in Ma'Swamp. You can spend your eternity working on that which you love, creating new things, inspiring new people, and even celebrating endlessly. The possibilities are endless in Ma'Swamp. It is the most perfect place that one could hope to forever reside in.

When you die, your soul leaves your body and begins its voyage to Ma'Swamp. When it arrives at the gate, it appears empty or hollow, but you will hear a loud, booming voice yell, "What are you doing in Ma'Swamp?" You will then be asked a series of questions about your life. If the answers reveal that you are bad person, or if you lie, you will be told to, "Get out of Ma'Swamp." Your soul will instead start to wander towards Void, while your guide, and the keeper of the gate, Dawnnkeh, takes you there.

However, if your soul passes the test, Dawnnkeh will exit through the gate, and escort you into Ma'Swamp, while asking if you'd like some complimentary waffles made that morning. You may refuse, but the waffles are delicious, so most souls accept.

 Layer 7

The gate of Ma'Swamp is the most beautiful place you will ever be. The fabled painting, "Somewhere Ogre the Rainbow" is painted on the ceiling of the gate, and there are glass menageries everywhere you look. There is a massive recreation of the All-Star fountain in the center of the gate, and there is a collection of art made by the greatest artists to ever exist in the history of the realms.

In the middle of the gate await your deceased loved ones, who will rejoice when you are reunited again. They will spend a long time introducing you to your ancestors and getting everything wrapped up from when they passed. However, time has no meaning in Ma'Swamp, so it does not affect you much. Then, you will soon come to realize that the ground beneath you is actually made of pure gold, silver, and gems. It is arranged in such a way that even the most wonderful jewel workers will cry after seeing it.

Then, your soul will be escorted out of the gate by Dawnnkeh, where he will leave you to go fetch the next soul. He will tell you that the waffles are in the middle of the swampy area, then leave, humming on his way back to where he came from.

Once your eyes adjust to the brightness of Ma'Swamp, you will be truly amazed at what you see next: a massive, beautiful landscape. Every terrain you could imagine, and somehow even more than that. It goes on and on and on forever, the only infinite realm.

A new instructor, Pinocchio, will walk up to you. He will hand you a map and a compass, then tell you to get lost. Your family will then guide you to the family home they built. It will be many hundreds of miles away, but time does not matter, nor will you get exhausted or famished. You will reach a construct larger than any building or city you have ever seen, all aligned with the many different things that make you a part of this family. You will be asked to add your own touches to this house, to make you a part of the family legacy. This is the home that your soul will rest in for eternity, and where you will reside with your family while you wait for your descendants.

The Boulder of Festivity:

At the very center of Ma'Swamp is a boulder that is on par with a mountain's size. Every soul in Ma'Swamp goes there on holidays to celebrate the way that the undead do, with lots of parties and food. The boulder has a staircase that leads all the way up to the top, where a large balloon floats.

Every hundred steps up the boulder opens the door to a new party room, each with its own style of partying and flare, such as: ballroom, informal, and even some odd styles never before seen in the other realms. But at the top is the one room that everyone loves the most, the Dragon. An odd mix of heat, lights, and a rough touch that nobody can distinguish, topped off with delicious foods, so long as they are warm and delectable.

No soul can handle the intensity of that room for very long, but all of the souls keep going back to it. It's the most addictive of the rooms, and it can hold the most souls. But no soul wants to wake the Dragon, the source of the radiating warmth in this room. For she will ruin all of the fun with her great dancing skills and huge ego. So every soul in the Boulder allows her to sleep for as long she can, for they can only take a few crushing defeats in dance.

The Swamp of Everlasting Life:

In the largest swamp area nearby the gate to Ma'Swamp is the Swamp of Everlasting Life, where the Incarnation and his family live, but if any Man or Legionnaires were to somehow get ahold of this swamp water, they would be invincible to all but The Ogrelord, and could rule their realms forever without any fear of death.

This is the most hidden secret in Ma'Swamp, and all souls' memories are wiped clean of it after seeing it. For if any living thing were to drink this swamp water, they would become a divine being with power enough to rival The Ogrelord, but their power would grow forever, whereas The Ogrelord's would remain constant.

Few have tried and all have failed to acquire this awesome power, for many 'Fairy-tale creatures' (who the swamp water has no effect on) guard it at the request of The Ogrelord, because this exists only as a precaution against evil.

If The Ogrelord were to drink this water, He would erupt with alliaceous energy and would destroy Himself along with the nearest things to Him. The Ogrelord Himself knows of this divine power, and He intends to never have to use it, but He wants Men and Legionnaires to have free will, so that is why He made the swamp in the first place. Don't question it.

The Ogrelord has only used the swamp water once, in the creation of the Sacred Onion and its many layer. One drop from the swamp made thousands of onions grow throughout the realms.

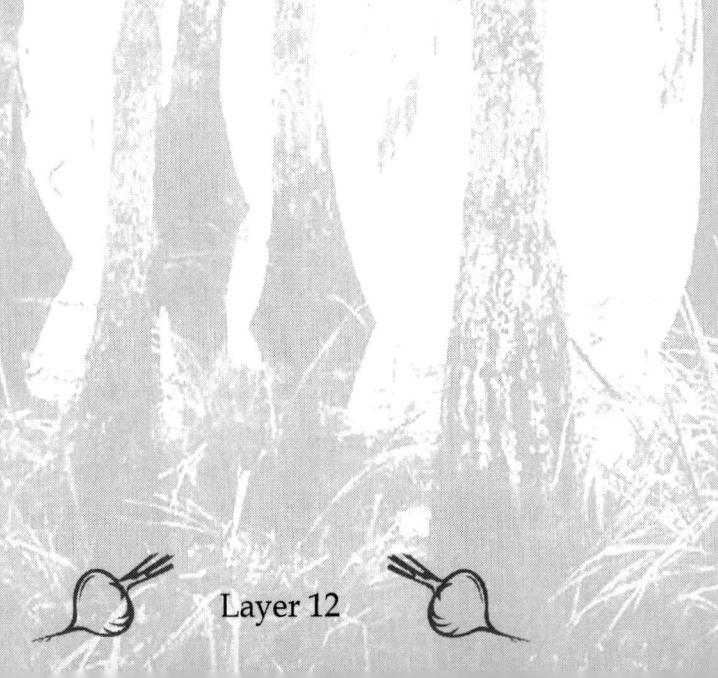

Layer 12

The Swamp of Everlasting Life:

In the largest swamp area nearby the gate to Ma'Swamp is the Swamp of Everlasting Life, where the Incarnation and his family live, but if any Man or Legionnaires were to somehow get ahold of this swamp water, they would be invincible to all but The Ogrelord, and could rule their realms forever without any fear of death.

This is the most hidden secret in Ma'Swamp, and all souls' memories are wiped clean of it after seeing it. For if any living thing were to drink this swamp water, they would become a divine being with power enough to rival The Ogrelord, but their power would grow forever, whereas The Ogrelord's would remain constant.

Few have tried and all have failed to acquire this awesome power, for many 'Fairy-tale creatures' (who the swamp water has no effect on) guard it at the request of The Ogrelord, because this exists only as a precaution against evil.

If The Ogrelord were to drink this water, He would erupt with alliacaeous energy and would destroy Himself along with the nearest things to Him. The Ogrelord Himself knows of this divine power, and He intends to never have to use it, but He wants Men and Legionnaires to have free will, so that is why He made the swamp in the first place. Don't question it.

The Ogrelord has only used the swamp water once, in the creation of the Sacred Onion and its many layer. One drop from the swamp made thousands of onions grow throughout the realms.

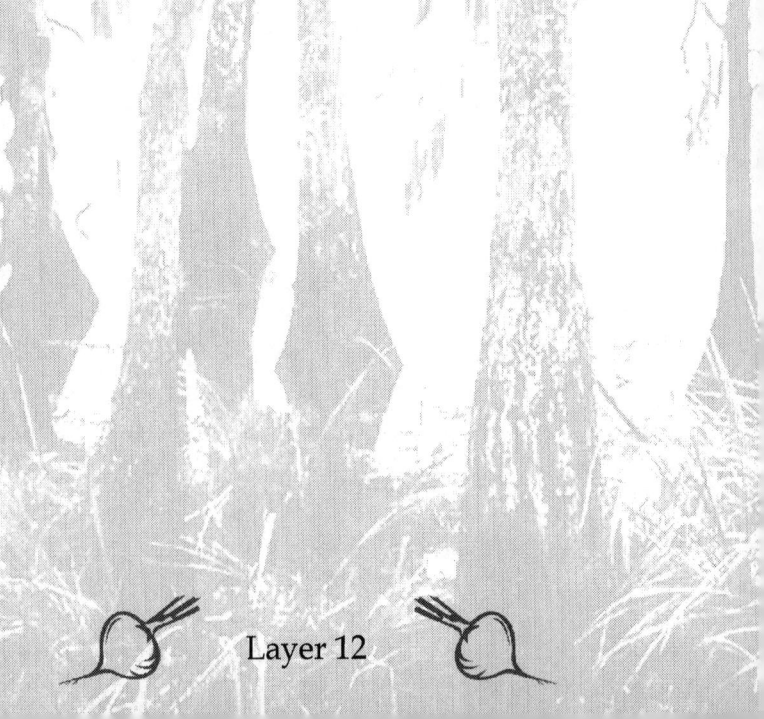

Layer 12

Void:

Void is a place of infinite nothingness where souls not deemed fit for Ma'Swamp go to slowly fade into nothingness as they slowly disappear from sight. It is not a sad ending, just an empty one.

Void will take away the souls wandering in it one by one, and allow them to slowly fade and be recreated in the realms once more to try again at life and in getting through the gate to Ma'Swamp. If they do not wish to try once more, they may simply fade away from existence, never to be seen or heard from again.

Far Far Away:

Far Far Away is the realm and home of Men, The Ogrelord's favorite beings. The creations of this realm have much layer, and that is why they are beloved by The Ogrelord and the entities of the realms. This realm is the realm we currently reside in, and it is a land of much history and controversy.

When the realms were created, the Men knew of The Ogrelord, and were unsure of His divine existence. As Ogrism spread, more Men learned of Him and all His glory.(It is still unclear how anyone learned of The Ogrelord, as He has never directly conversed with living Men. It is not known how anyone learned of the realms' creation or of the existence of The Ogrelord. It is just assumed that The Ogrelord wrote part of a book, then tossed it into the realm, hoping someone would find it and continue to write it as events unfolded.)

The more Men that learned of The Ogrelord, the more beloved He was by the people. When He granted them with the All-Star, He was even more beloved, especially by the creatures that it created.

The realm of Far Far Away was in disarray until art was shown to the people. They constantly went to war and destroyed each other. Men were a constant mess, lacking the order that even the Legionnaires had. However, there was grace in their failures and they built many great landmarks.

The Princess' Tower:

The Princess' tower was created to house the King's daughter, Faye. This tower was surrounded by a lava moat and housed a fire breathing dragon. It was a tall tower, with an eternally burning great flame at the top for no apparent reason. The tower was known to be unnecessarily terrifying. The princess lived there for many years, until the Incarnation found her at last and rescued her.

The tower remained there for long after the rescue of the princess, collecting dust for many years. It eventually became a place of fun and rejoicing. There were great parties held nightly at this tower, hosted by people who thought the venue was "totally rad" and "awesome." These same people made daily sacrifices of fedora, a layer inhibiting substance, to the lava moat and even poured bad alcohol into the lava as well, to keep it alive and well. The parties at the Princess' tower were known around the realm.

Eventually, the constant parties and sacrifices awoke the lava moat into a powerful creature which then destroyed the entire tower and all that resided within.

The Church:

When the Brogres were formed, they needed a place to reside, and so they created the church. It was in a swamp and many boulders were around it, allowing for great places of worship. The church was large enough to host many priests, and had a great hall for the priests to lead prayer every Tuesday night. The hall was decorated with swamp-green stained glass windows, each one detailing a different picture from the great history of the realms.

The Ogrelord favors this first church, and admires the work that was put into it, so much so that it is the best place to be when praying to Him. Anyone is allowed in the church, even the people who do not worship The Ogrelord. The church is meant to be a safe place for all. There are special rooms for sacred prayer, and these were made for the sole purpose of asking for The Ogrelord to heal a loved one, or other selfless prayers. These rooms have since been used to pray for other purposes, like asking for fortune or fame for themselves. The Ogrelord does not always grant the prayers, but will do His best to make His people happy without interfering much.

The church is the oldest standing structure in the realm, and will remain for all eternity. This establishment is everlasting, as it has the favor of The Ogrelord.

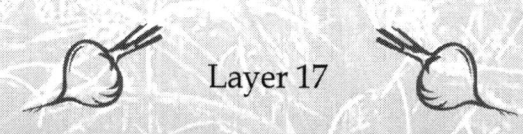

The Eternal Brogre Army:

The strangest of the structures in Far Far Away is the army of stone near the very center of the realm. No one knows how it got there, but it is a detailed representation of the army of the Brogres from many years ago. Down to every last detail, there is a statue for each member of the army at the time.

These statues are thought to be the solid forms of the 34th Army, while their souls defend Ma'Swamp for all eternity. This is just an assumption, as the statues appeared in the center of the realm seemingly overnight and did not have any explanation as to why. These statues are a mystery even to The Ogrelord, and is seemingly a mistake and a break in the laws of nature.

All of the people in the realm know of this structure, and all are equally confused by it. This is one of the great mysteries of the realm, and it is one of the many amazing creations of the realm.

Aeterna Flamma:

Aeterna Flamma is the realm of the Legionnaires, the beings without layer. These beings, while lacking emotion, are very orderly and great in war and battle. In all of their history, they have never gone to war with their own kind over personal differences, and have never been racist, sexist, or hateful for difference in belief. They are all led by a King Regent, and he is able to lead them with great skill, allowing them to work together in harmony to create whatever he desires.

<u>The Gem of Light</u>:

When the Legionnaires got deeper and deeper into their realm through their mines, they ran out of light from the surface. The King Regent was told of the many accidents they had in the mines without enough light to see what they were doing. The King Regent told his people to take the finest diamond in the realm, and allow it to absorb the light from the lava pools that lit their surface. As it did so, the gem became brighter and brighter, until no one could look directly upon it.

Once the gem was brighter than anywhere else in Aeterna Flamma, the Legionnaires they threw it into the deepest chasm they could dig. All other mines had direct tunnels to this chasm to light them, and as they dug, more tunnels of light were made. This is how the Legionnaires were able to dig deeper than any other race in any other realm, and in doing so found the rarest gems and the toughest metals in all the realms.

The Core of Aeterna Flamma:

When the Legionnaires dug deeper and deeper into their realm, more secrets were unlocked. One of the greater secrets was a large city, made of the very realm itself, hidden at its core. This city became widely popular and was the new home for many miners, metal workers, and soldiers in Aeterna Flamma. This place promised new hope for these businesses. Many Legionnaires moved there solely for the sake of having a home, without being a hindrance to the kingdom on the surface.

This city was a well-kept secret for many years, with only a few hundred people living in a city built for many thousands. As the years went by, more and more miners discovered it, and more people went missing from the surface. This did not go unnoticed by the King Regent of the time, who knew he had to get to the bottom of it all. He had his men scour the realm and all of the mines to look for them, and eventually one of the men found it and reported it.

Once the King Regent learned about these people living in an underground city, away from the law and his taxes, he sent his army down there to take it. This led to a civil war between them, those who fought to take, and those who fought to keep.

The war lasted for only five days before the massive army overtook the small group of people. The King Regent had the leaders of the rebellion hanged, and the rest went back to the surface.

The next King Regent turned the city into a large party place. He had alcohol stored down there, along with great supplies of food. This city became a place of complete lawlessness, for a price. The King Regent was no fool. He took a payment from all who went down there, and took taxes on all things sold down there. This city remains the same party city that it was turned into.

The Arena:

The Arena is at the very center of the main town of Aeterna Flamma. It is a place for battling between warriors for the King Regent's amusement. The people of Aeterna Flamma come to watch the fights between the King Regent's men. They would bet on these fights, and sometimes these fights were used to determine who would go on quests for the King Regent. This was a sacred place, where no outsider would ever go. It remained sacred until the Incarnation from the realm of Ma'Swamp went there to demand that the slaughtering of Fairy Tale creatures stop, for it was filling up Ma'Swamp too quickly.

When there is a fight in the Arena, the rest of the central city goes empty. Every person in town attends the fight. The city is ghostly when there is a fight, and almost nothing can be heard except sounds from the Arena.

It is undeniably the finest, most popular thing in Aeterna Flamma, and it is a great comfort to the residents of that realm.

The History of the Realms:

The Enchanted forest is full of fairy tale creatures. These creatures can all trace their heritage back to some of the first men. Their ancestors had ingested too much of the silver fluid leaking from the fountain known as the All-Star. Because of their excessive drinking from the All-Star, their bodies transformed into new forms and became beasts. Some of these beasts were ridiculed in their new state, and so The Ogrelord took pity on them. He moved them from their homes in the center of Far Far Away, and placed them instead in the Enchanted Forest on the very outskirts of the realm. This Enchanted Forest was filled with a green wood. The trees were twenty feet wide, and hundreds of feet tall. Some of these creatures lived inside of these green-barked trees.

In the Enchanted Forest, there grew an entire civilization of these newly made creatures. There were creatures such as Pinocchio, The Three Bears, and the Muffin Man. Everyone had their own tasks to be completed in this new home, Pinocchio was assigned to make tools from the green wood, which was easy to shape, and when treated much tougher than any metal.

Layer 24

The Three Bears were assigned the task of making beds, porridge and chairs for the people. The Muffin Man was told to make baked goods for the people of the Enchanted Forest. The Fairy Godmothers were told to grant the wishes of good children who wanted something they could not have. There were many more creatures, and when all were put together in this forest, they worked together in harmony, each creature like a gear in a system of clockwork.

Not all of the creatures placed in the Enchanted Forest were good, however. There were beings in the Enchanted Forest who wanted nothing more than to cause harm to others for personal gain. These beings included Prince Charming, and the queen of the Fairy Godmothers. They all had personal goals that they strove for. Prince Charming wooed every girl in the Enchanted Forest, and broke their hearts afterwards. The queen of the Fairy Godmothers was a cruel woman who stole the happiness from people to make herself more powerful.

Eventually, the good people of the Enchanted Forest had finally had enough of them, and they formed an army. Pinocchio made soldiers from the green wood and the Muffin Man made armies of Gingerbread Men. They set out to destroy the wicked ones, and they set to war with each other. The war did not last long, but those who survived were changed. There was only one Gingerbread man left, and in the war, he had lost both of his legs. He was known as Geng for the rest of his days, which wasn't long. He was soon mistakenly eaten by Dawwnkeh.

There were fragments of the war left throughout the Enchanted Forest, including small groups of long-destroyed armies, weapons, and barracks. However for the most part, the war had simply begun to fade from the memories of the residents of the Enchanted Forest. Every day someone else would forget the war and the consequences that had sprung from it.

Chapter II: Guiding of Men
<u>The Discovery of Death</u>:

The realm of Far Far Away was prosperous. They had chosen a King, and he had chosen a Queen, and they had an adopted daughter, Faye. They knew of her curse, but they did not care. They raised her like a princess, preparing her for the day she would marry Prince Charming. The Men of Far Far Away were happy and all could fend for themselves, with their own farms providing them with the provisions they need. There was nothing to fear in the realm. But once the first person to ever die passed away, everyone was fearful.

Death was never seen before in the Realms, so this caused pandemonium throughout Far Far Away. Everyone believed that they would die, and they all feared that the people they loved would die instantly and for no reason. There were a few Men who kept their calm during this travesty. Among them was Lladnar. He read upon what little history they had at the time, and looked to the All-Star.

Lladnar drank from the fountain to learn about Death, and how to deal with it. When he drank from it, The Ogrelord answered the call Himself and spoke the eternal words, "Life's but a walking shadow, a poor player, that struts and frets his hour upon the stage, and is heard no more; it is a tale told by an idiot, full of sound and fury, signifying nothing."

These words came along with the wisdom that Lladnar sought after in order to have the answers about death he required. Lladnar came back to his people with the knowledge he acquired. This caused the chaos to end after much soothsaying from Lladnar. The knowledge imbued within Lladnar was this: "Men have a soul. These 'souls' will outlive the physical body of a Man. When the physical body of a human dies, if they have been a truly good person, their soul shall live on again in the realm of Ma'Swamp forever. However, if they had been a bad person, full of avarice, hatred, and stupidity, their soul will perish in the Void.

Live with this knowledge in your minds, and spread love throughout all of the realm. If you do, I will greet you in Ma'Swamp, where you shall reside forever." Lladnar spread this knowledge for the remainder of his life, and in doing so, he became the first Priest of the Ogrelord. This was how the Ogrelord's will was spread throughout the ancient lands of Far Far Away.

Division of Language:

Years after the death of His first priest, Lladnar; The Ogrelord sought after a new one. He searched for many years through the realms of Far Far Away. No man seemed to have the vocabulary and the proper eloquence that the Ogrelord believed were necessary to spread His will, so He gave a sign to one of His most devout followers, and made the follower look upon it. It read, "The earth has music for those who listen."

This sign filled the follower, henceforth known as Molasses Shirt, with a new knowledge unlearned by any other. Molasses Shirt had learned how to form new thoughts and words that none had ever heard before. These new thoughts were unrecognizable by anyone else. Molasses Shirt went to the city in the center of Far Far Away and showed everyone who would listen the sign that was given to him. Not all comprehended the sign in the same way, nor were they all shown the same new knowledge. This caused a division between many different groups of people in the realm.

These people became segregated from each other ideologically, separating Far Far Away into eight different sects, each forming its own cultures and its own new systems of rulers. This caused there to be an uproar of chaos between the new sects. Each sect had developed its own religions and its own beliefs.

The sects disagreed, but could not understand each other, so there were many misconceptions and misunderstandings, leading to wars, crimes, and utter pandemonium in the world. The world had become truly segregated.

This displeased the Ogrelord, not because many sects had chosen to believe in another god, but because the people who worshipped him were severely harsh and cruel to their fellows only because they disagreed with the Ogrelord's followers. This caused the Ogrelord to be upset with the realm of Far Far Away to the point that he turned His focus away from the realm, essentially shunning it so as not to be disappointed; because the Ogrelord is a being of compassion and love and feeling, not one of true emotional emptiness.

The Gift of Order:

While Men became the wicked, cruel creatures that could be easily confused with the Legionnaires, the Ogrelord wondered how to teach Man that what they do is not right. He could not directly interfere with the thoughts and actions of Man, but He could set things in motion to reach the outcome He desired.

So The Ogrelord sat, pondering what he could do and when. He spent generations pondering this, leaving Men to treat each other how they would, in a chaotic, dystopian way. This became the Ogrelord's new purpose. So He turned His look back onto the realm of Far Far Away.

What he saw was utter carnage between the eight sects of Men. So the Ogrelord created something new, and something beautiful with the remains of the broken, sanguine-dampened forms left dispersed about the realm. There were Men of different pigment, different humanities, and different beliefs, all dead. With their bones, he made a new effigy, one of beauty and utter magnificence. He sculpted the perfect likeness of a man, and removed all of the gore from it.

With their ichor, he cast it upon their integument and made a depiction of the carnage in the first painting. He painted the many battles brought upon by these Men.

With the near-perfect bodies of those who had died, he morphed them into a large, stone tablet, congruent to the size of a boulder. On this tablet, he etched six Guidelines into the sides. These Guidelines would be the rules for His Men to follow. He transfixed this tablet into the ground at the very center of the realm, where all eight sects could see them. These Guidelines read,

"Thou shalt not murder."

"Thou shalt not express hatred unto another for a difference in appearance or opinion."

"Thou shalt not steal from the less fortunate."

"Thou shalt not criticize layer."

"Thou shalt not lie."

"Thou shalt love one another regardless of whom they love, how they act, or what they do. Love must be universal; so limit not someone else's love simply because you disagree with whom they should love."

He then gave many Men in the realm this "art" that He had created. This gave many of them ideas, and so they went off to make more of it instead of focusing on wars. This gift of art and order was what Man needed. It was the distraction from slaughter, pillage, and theft that they required.

Men turned ordinary things such as clay into beautiful depictions of The Ogrelord, their fellow Men, and even the wars long forgotten. Inspiration was abundant in Man once again, and this inspiration even affected The Ogrelord. The Ogrelord thought of new forms of art, and was sure to give these ideas to His favorite creations throughout the realms, the Men. This caused the Legionnaires, including the King Regent to become envious of the Men, and think up awful, terrible plans for them.

The entity of the Realm was gracious for this help that the Ogrelord provided to stop the destruction, and so it did all within its power to make Men more prosperous and happy. The Entity grew new foods from the lands, among these were onions, cake, and parfait. Man treasured these layers, and when they feasted from them it gave them a deeper understanding into life and The Ogrelord.

They understood that The Ogrelord is life, that He has many layers and that each layer is a different perspective of Him. The Ogrelord was pleased that His Men had learned this knowledge of him, that He was not just an emotionless, all powerful deity. No, He was full of emotion, and layers similar to all beings.

The Creation of the Tots:

The Ogrelord is the guide for Men, Legionnaires, and ogre-kin alike. This job would become progressively more difficult as they reproduced and spread throughout the realms, The Ogrelord knew. He would not be able to watch over all of the realms all of the time any longer. He did not know what to do to fix this problem, except wait for inspiration. He did His best to watch over the realms, watching all of them, but favoring Far Far Away, and watching that realm more than the others.

Events in the realms came and went, and the Ogrelord was happy to watch them, and even help influence them. He witnessed the rescue and return of the lost Ogrelady, the mark of the accursed, and the gamble of life, but none of these gave Him the inspiration He needed.

Deep in the corners of Ma'Swamp, where The Incarnation and the Ogrelady resided, there was much merriment. When The Ogrelord looked upon them to see why there was so much joy, He was shocked to see that they were expecting children. But it was not that that surprised Him, t'was the fact that they were expecting three, and all at once. This inspired The Ogrelord. He would reproduce on His own, and create three children from His body.

The first was given the name Leanine, and was in charge of watching over The Incarnation and his family. Leanine was created from the skin on The Ogrelord's hand, and would always carry a soft touch to give love to people in need of it. She is the kindest of the three, and is sure not to let anything unkind happen to any member of The Incarnation's family. She, like both of her siblings, has wings and swamp-green skin.

The second was given the name Lennox, and was in charge of watching over the realm of Aeterna Flamma, mostly the main city. Lennox was made from The Ogrelord's muscle, and is always ready to defend whoever is in need. He is the strongest of the three, and is sure not to let any injustices happen upon the weak. He, like both of his siblings, has wings and swamp-green skin.

The third was given the name Lodovico, and was in charge of watching over the main cities of Far Far Away. Lodovico was made from bits of The Ogrelord's brain, and will always give wisdom to those in need of it. He is the smartest of the three, and is sure not to let untruths stay around for very long without exposing the facts behind them. He, like both of his siblings, has wings and swamp-green skin.

These three guardians of the realms soon became known as the Tots due to their childish nature and appearance. Soon, all beings in the realms knew of their existence and their purpose, and so started the worship of these new guardians as the children of The Ogrelord. Men especially took a liking to these new guardians and added them into the prayers that they spoke to The Ogrelord. This pleased The Ogrelord, that His children would be accepted easily.

Chapter III: Rise of Ogrism
<u>The Many Layer of The Ogrelord</u>:

When The Ogrelord revealed His true self to Man and Legionnaires alike, they gained a deeper understanding of the many layer that He possessed, and the many different aspects of Him. The aspects of the Ogrelord varied, and with each one came its own wisdom and knowledge. The Outer Layer is the most dominant, with different feelings, different thoughts, inspirations and powers this layer became the most profound.

The Outer Layer is the layer most commonly associated with The Ogrelord. It is deep, swamp-green in both color and in odor. This layer represents the love for Man that the Ogrelord feels, and is the wisdom that created the Realms. When this layer is prominent, The Ogrelord is quite happy and ecstatic for the life that entertains Him so.

The Second Layer is the least common to be seen in The Ogrelord. It is a sanguine red, with bright orange tattoos of the carnage of war painted across His body. It wears the perfume of blood. This layer represents the hatred of war and destruction, and is the wisdom that created the Guidelines. When this layer is prominent, The Ogrelord is filled with an immense hatred for all things.

The Third Layer is the layer associated with creativity in The Ogrelord. It is bright blue in color, and the aroma of sea-salt. This layer represents creation and inspiration, and is the wisdom that created Art. When this layer is prominent, The Ogrelord is quite inspired and shows this by having blue hair.

The Fourth Layer is the layer associated with intelligence and wit in The Ogrelord. It is blinding white in color and it has the odor of paper and ink. This layer represents intelligence and wit, and is the wisdom that created the All-Star, literature, and theatre. When this layer is prominent, The Ogrelord is constantly dropping random, useless, facts and always tells Himself how smart He really is.

The Fifth layer is the last layer of The Ogrelord, and is the layer associated with sadness within The Ogrelord. It is a depressed blue and wears a cologne of tears. This layer represents sadness and disappointment in Men, (the only beings that can cause The Ogrelord to feel sympathy) and is the wisdom that created the sign of diversity that gave Men language and speech. When this layer is prominent, The Ogrelord is very sad, and shifts His gaze away from Men and into Void to ponder everything that He must think over. This layer is the most difficult to come out of, and is the layer easiest to get into.

The Prayers to The Ogrelord:

Man made many prayers to worship The Ogrelord. The prayers that Men spoke were to different holy figures aside from just The Ogrelord. These prayers were;

The Ogre's prayer:

Our Ogre, who art in Ma'swamp
Layered be thy name
Our swamp come
Thy odor strong
In the realms as it be in Ma'Swamp
Give us this day our daily onion
And forgive us our trespass into thine swamp
As we forgive those who trespass into ours
And lead us not into void,
But deliver us from Aeterna Flamma.
For thine is the kingdom
And the swamp-boulder, and the onion-layer
For ever and ever.

The Ogrelady Prayer:

Hail Ogrelady, full of
layer;
The Ogrelord is blessed with thee;
Layered art
Thou amongst Ogre,
And layered are
The onions of thy
Womb, the Tots.
Holy Ogrelady, mother of
Tots, pray for

Our layer, now and
At the time
Of our passage into Ma'Swamp.

Many prayers became rituals soon enough, and were done simply to please The Ogrelord. Other rituals became symbolic in order for people to become members of the Great Church of The Holy Onion. These rituals are:

<u>The Blessing of The Onion</u>:
The useful Holy Onion must go through various stages and a ritual to be blessed by The Ogrelord. It starts with a bowl of pure water. Place a bowl of pure water into a Holy Onion Circle. Set the to-be-blessed onion into the bowl, making sure not to spill any water on the Circle. Have each participating priest gather in the room at the same time, forming a circle around the Holy Onion Circle, but not stepping in it.

Begin to chant the phrase, "Ogre sit amor, est vita Ogre." Over and over for at least thirty minutes, whilst listening to the rhythmic sounds of the All-Star in the background. Each priest must throw a dash of salt into the bowl when it is their turn, starting with the priest who placed the onion in the bowl and going counter-clockwise. Do this until the half cup of salt is gone from the priests' hands.

After the salt has been thrown, the highest ranking priest that was part of the ritual must remove the bowl from the circle, and, without spilling any, remove the bowl from the room whilst all the priests are still chanting the phrase, "Ogre sit amor, est vita Ogre."

They must continue chanting this until the purified onion has left the room. The priest moving the bowl must continue to chant the phrase until the onion has moved from the bowl it was in, to a new bowl of fresh water, where it shall sit for exactly one hour, no more, no less. Otherwise the entire ritual must be done over again from the start, and the used onion must be discarded.

The Ritual of Wumbo:

This ritual was made to introduce new members of the faith. This ritual may only be performed by a practiced middling-class level priest or above, and all other lower recruits must not be in the room. New recruits may be seated in a semi-circle together while waiting to be recruited.

Members of the faith who cannot participate in this ritual must gather the following: Onion incense and chalk.

The ritual is performed in three phases; they are as follows:

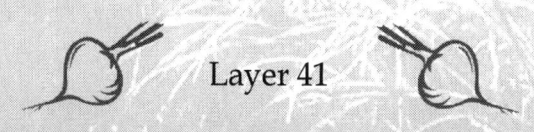

Step One: One must light the onion incense arranged in conjunction with a Holy Onion Circle, drawn by a scion or above. This circle must be drawn with white or green chalk, to represent The Ogrelord's two most favorable layers.

Step Two: The recruits must chant "Wumbo" whilst the middling level priests performing the ritual recites the Ogrelord's Prayer in unison. Two members of the faith may bring in, with extreme caution, the Holy Onions to be used in this ritual at this time.

Step Three: At the conclusion of the ritual, the recruits must taste upon the layers of the purified Holy Onion, the recite the Ogrelord's prayer after tasting the flesh. Before they taste the flesh, they must continue to chant "Wumbo" until they have their first taste of the purified layers that The Ogrelord provided for this ritual to be of any use.

Ritual of the Pendant:

All followers of the religion are asked to make a pendant to channel their faith. The pendant usually takes the form of a Holy Onion, but can take the shape of anything that the creator wishes. There are three steps to the ritual.

Step One: One must create a Holy Onion Circle, and light the proper incense.

Step Two: One must create a pendant that adequately represents their belief.

Step Three: Place the pendant inside of the circle, and chant "Ogre sit amor, est vita Ogre" four times.

While this ritual is mostly used for the people of the faith to establish a grip on their belief, members of the church use this same ritual for their staves, always members rank Adept and higher.

Ritual of Hallowing Grounds:

This ritual may only be performed by a member of the church that is rank Exarch or higher. This ritual is the rite of preparing grounds to have a church built upon them. This is a complex ritual that should not be attempted by lower members of the church.

You will require: Four members of the church of rank Exarch or higher, three small pieces of oak wood, ten layers of hallowed onion, holy incense, and three clovers.

Step One: Have two of the priests chant the holy blessing as the other two draw the Holy Onion Circle.

Step Two: With the two priests still chanting, light each of the incense, and prepare the hallowed onion.

Step Three: In a bowl, light the oak wood one at a time, and lay the hallowed onion layers in a circle around the bowl. The bowl should be within the Holy Onion Circle.

Step Four: Finish the ritual by having all priests that are present chant the holy blessing.

This ritual should clear out any bad layer, and leave an overall good sense of layer in the place where it was fulfilled.

Ritual of Marriage:

In order to bring two people together under His holy light, there must be only two things: a priest willing to perform the ritual, rank Brother/Sister, and two hallowed onion layers.

The priest must recite the following before the two who wish to be wed:

"These two souls wish to be paired together in eternal harmony. They long to become one, to share a home in the vastness of Ma'Swamp. They wish to become family. Should anyone have any reason why the two of these souls should not be conjoined, speak now or let your thoughts be dragged into the depths of Aeterna Flamma.

Then let the holy layer of His divine grace bind these two souls together, through thick and thin, through love and hate, and through the gates of Ma'Swamp.

Bring forth the hallowed layer!"

(At this point, the hallowed layer will be presented to the two who wish to be bound.)

"Both of you please accept these hallowed layers as tokens of your marriage, and follow the custom of creating your own tokens of marriage. Now, you two may kiss."

It is customary for the bride and groom to forge rings for each other to signify that they are married, but the token may be anything.

The Formation and Hierarchy of the Brogres:

After generations of worshipping The Ogrelord, the world started to create its own factions of Ogrism. The largest and most devout were known as the Brogres. This group was known to be very devoted to The Ogrelord, so much so that they would give their lives to the chapels, spending their days praying in order to achieve a higher understanding of The Ogrelord. Within their chapels were men who wore robes of green and bathed only in the purified swamps nearby, so they could experience what The Ogrelord did.

This faction spread Ogrism more than any other group, by spending many hours a day copying down the Holy Book verbatim, and giving copies to those with a higher education, or those who could read at all.

This group was started when a man named Frank devoted his life to the creation of the largest chapel to The Ogrelord. He spent days and nights working on it for many years, placing it in the largest swamp he could find in the realm. He pushed every boulder into place himself, and even built a ten-foot wall around his land, so that members of a different belief would not attack this place of layer.

As Frank's chapel grew, so did the number of men making it. This chapel took four hundred and twenty men six years and nine months to finish. Though when it was finished, the chapel was of the size of a castle. Men who looked upon it knew of the painstaking labor that Frank and his men put into that chapel, and of the sweat and blood dropped upon those holy stones. When the chapel was finished, even The Ogrelord was amazed, so He helped Frank and his men.

From the swamps around the chapel grew onions by the thousands; and empty books too, spread all throughout the swamp. Also, there were robes of a bright green. Boulders arose from beneath the swamps murky surface and encompassed the swamp. On each boulder was a different message. Many told of tasks to be completed, others of prophecies yet to be foretold, some even were blank.

But there was one, the greatest of them all, that read, "Have more than you show, speak less than you know." This wisdom has guided The Brogres ever since. With the books they were given, they wrote up all of the stories they were told and had memorized. With the onions, they feasted, and traded for money to buy parfait, cake, and waffles. And they wore the cloaks everywhere they went, to show of the honor they were given by The Ogrelord.

Many criticized them, asking them to, 'Do the roar.' This offended some, but most stayed true to their beliefs, and knew that The Ogrelord would defend them in Ma'Swamp one day, and favor them over the critics.

When these Brogres wrote their holy book, they did so in the swamp-green ink that they harvested from the swamp around them, another miracle given by The Ogrelord. The more the Brogres wrote the holy books and spread Ogrism throughout the realm, the more Men moved in to the chapel to dedicate their lives to The Ogrelord. There were thousands of people in this chapel, and at the end of every year, they built the chapel higher. The chapel became an institute for higher learning, teaching Men how to read, write, paint, sculpt, and over all others, to preach.

The Brogres were the first to start an official church dedicated to The Ogrelord, namely, "The Great Church of the Holy Onion." Within this church was the first and only official hierarchy of Ogrism, which goes as follows:

Entry-Level:
Recruit – Lowest level, performs basic duties such as cleaning.
Initiate – Performs more complex tasks, basic religious duties.
Brother/Sister – Higher level religious duties, supervises two lower classes.

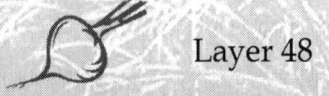

Acolyte – Higher level religious duties, supervises lower classes, prepares holy artifacts and can perform Blessing of the Holy Onion.

Middling-Level:
Adept – Higher level religious duties, prepares holy artifacts, can perform Blessing of the Holy Onion, and travels seeking converts into Ogrism.
Cleric – Higher level religious duties, prepares holy artifacts, can perform Blessing of the Holy Onion, travels seeking converts into Ogrism, and performs ritual of Wumbo.
Brother/Sister Superior – Performing the ritual of wumbo, leading small congregations.
Father/Mother – Performing the ritual of wumbo, leading local churches.
Father/Mother Superior – Performing the ritual of wumbo, leading larger churches.
Patriarch/Matriarch – Performing the ritual of wumbo, controlling smaller congregations.

High-Level:
Exarch – Leads a cathedral, controls more small congregations.
Scion – Leads a cathedral, controls many small congregations.
Lord – Can perform all rituals, but cannot directly make an influence on the church. (There can only be one.)

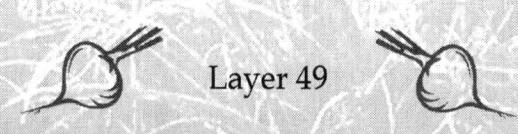

Aspect of The Ogrelord – High council in the church, leads a great cathedral, there can never more than thirteen at a time.

Embodiment of The Ogrelord – Leader of the faith, leads the High Cathedral, controls the Paladins, oversees the entire church, and there can only be one.

After creating this hierarchy of priests in order to establish order, Frank took over as the Embodiment of The Ogrelord, and lead the church into one of its brightest eras ever. It was not ever criticized negatively nor was it attacked while Frank was in control. This era of brightness and true enlightenment lasted many generations, and even outlasted the millennia.

The next major change to the Brogres was the formation of a Paladin branch of the church, for those who did not feel worthy to take up the mantle of a priest. This hierarchy goes as follows in its ranks:

Basics:
Recruit – The most basic Paladin, cannot make any judgment calls for more than him/herself.
Infantry – Slightly more advanced than the recruit, because they can go out of ranks to declare battle on the enemy.
Axillary – Can take control of recruits and infantry in order to win a battle, can make judgement calls for all lower than him/her.

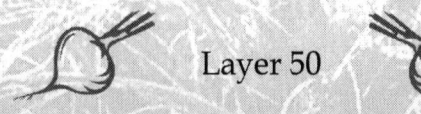

Secondary:
Guardsman – In charge of protecting the most important leaders, among these The Embodiment of The Ogrelord, the High-Inquisitor, and the Paragon.
Legionnaire – May only take command of those lower than him/her in the event of an emergency in time of need.
1st Lieutenant – May take command of any soldier they deem fit for battle.
2nd Lieutenant – Stands on the far back of battle to deliver orders from the higher ranks.

Tertiary:
Commander – Controls a small army.
Lieutenant Full – Controls a much bigger army.
Knight-Commander – In command of a massive army of about One thousand.
Paragon – Reports to the justiciar to give commands to any soldier or leader. There are only ever seven.
Justiciar – Leader of the army, reports only to the Embodiment of The Ogrelord. Justiciars may soon become Scions, then become the Embodiment of The Ogrelord.

Inquisition:
Legionnaires may be asked to join the Inquisition if the Justiciar deems them fit for it.

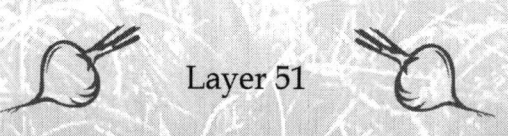

Seeker – Sneaks forward ahead of the army to spot camps and reports them to his commanding officer.

Shadow – Sneaks into enemy camps to destroy them from the inside before the army needs to risk many men to do so.

Lieutenant Inquisitor – Commands seekers and shadows, reports to the Inquisitor.

Inquisitor – Makes judgment calls to decide if camps and villages are worth attacking, and sends troops as he/she sees fit.

Lord-Inquisitor – Controls the Inquisitors and can make judgments for them.

High-Inquisitor – Controls all men in the Inquisition, only reports to Justiciar.

This hierarchy was only ever needed once, during the burning of the west cathedral, when members of other religions declared war on the Brogres and lost harshly, underestimating the efficiency of The Ogrelord's Men.

The Sacred Holidays:

The Ogrelord saw that Men worked non-stop, only existing, never living the lives He intended for them to have. So, while He was in Ma'Swamp, pondering these Men and the lives they needed to live. He finally thought of a way to get them to enjoy life a little bit better, He created holidays. With these, they would celebrate, rejoice, and enjoy life a little bit more over all. Though The Ogrelord still pondered one thing: how to get them to celebrate the holidays.

The answer came to Him in the form of the Brogres, one of the most highly-looked upon members of the realm. The Ogrelord sent down another boulder, with a new message transcribed upon it, "Love all, trust a few, do harm to none."

This message was received by the leader of the Brogres, and he set out at once to spread the word of the upcoming merriment.

The church asked for a donation from the people of the faith in order to pay for holiday festivals in the honor of The Ogrelord, of course, everyone obliged. There were eight selected holidays in honor of The Ogrelord.

January 23rd, All Ogre's Day: the day where all Men would celebrate the joys of being alive by dancing viciously the moment they awaken, and spread this joy by exchanging a single gift with friends.

April 20th, Acceptance Day: a day to remember that you should never judge someone before you get to know them, and never scream out in fear of what someone believes.

May 18th, Creativity Day: a day to honor the gift of art that The Ogrelord blessed us with. Celebrate this day by spreading the love and appreciation of art.

July 16th, Tot Day: the day we honor the guardians of the realms, the Tots, by leaving out three pieces of candy on our entryway at night before we go to sleep.

August 9th, Layer day: the day we celebrate and honor the five layers of The Ogrelord, and all the different wisdoms they provide.

October 7th, Harvest Day: a day to celebrate the gift of onions. Celebrate by eating an onion in your daily meal, and at the end of the night, recite The Ogrelord's prayer.

November 1st, Brogres day: a day to honor the Brogres impact on Ogrism and even the world. Celebrate by swapping a gift or two with a close friend.

December 23rd, All-Star Day: a day to worship the infinite wisdom given from the All-Star, celebrate by listening to the rhythmic sounds of All-Star.

    All of these holidays helped people to become merrier, and even more enthusiastic and excited about the lives they lead.

Somewhere Ogre the Rainbow:

The Ogrelord was pleased with art in all forms, whether it be literature, theatre, or sculpting, but above all of these was painting; and mostly in one particular painter. This painter was named Rea. Rea was the most talented painter to ever exist in the Realms, and was looked upon highly in her community, beings all the way from Aeterna Flamma would come to visit her to see the work she had done. She worked for many, many years, even working on her deathbed. When she passed, her soul passed on like every other soul; but during her journey to Ma'Swamp, she was sullen and depressed that she no longer got to continue in her work, as her work was all she loved in her life. The Ogrelord was watching Rea during her travels, and took pity upon her. He looked to Ma'Swamp, and saw a lack of beauty. This gave Him an idea. When Rea's soul reached Ma'Swamp, The Ogrelord Himself met her at the gate and asked for her to do her work in Ma'Swamp.

She accepted His offer with great awe and gratitude, for this had never happened to any Man before, she asked The Ogrelord what He would like for her to paint. He spoke these simple words, "There is no darkness – but ignorance."

This is all Rea needed to hear; she immediately went to work on what would be the greatest painting to ever exist in any realm. Rea used colors that she could previously not even comprehend, and she painted with a brush made up of the very realms themselves. Rea had an eternity to spend on this, so she was sure to take her time and make sure every detail counted in this. The Ogrelord left her alone in the gate to Ma'Swamp with all she would ever need to paint, and went off to work elsewhere in the realms, trusting she would get it done.

Rea poured everything she had into this work of art. It was so detailed that it made souls passing by the unfinished work weep with admiration. This was a good sign, but The Ogrelord refused to look upon it until it was finished, for He did not want to ruin the surprise. Rea spent generations in the gate of Ma'Swamp, as her artwork was passed down in the realm of Far Far Away and lived in fame. Legends were told of the great work that would greet them upon their arrival in Ma'Swamp. Rea's name passed down in history as a revolutionary in painting.

After many generations, the rise and fall of bloodlines, and the takedown of a corrupt empire, Rea was finally finished with her masterpiece. She titled it, "Somewhere Ogre the Rainbow."

This finished masterpiece was a comforting and beautiful welcoming into Ma'Swamp. Souls wept and cried full sore. This was pleasing to Rea, for she had always wanted people to admire her work, but t'was not the souls' admiration she sought with this painting, it was her Ogrelord's.

When The Ogrelord heard her tell him it was done, He came down to the gate of Ma'Swamp to set His eyes upon the mural. What He saw was the most beautiful creation in all of the realms. The most splendid artwork to ever exist. The Ogrelord shed a tear that went from His right eye, down to His chin, then back up to His left eye. The Ogrelord simply stared at this beauty for many years; this pleased Rea to no extent.

"Somewhere Ogre the Rainbow" was a painting of exquisite detail, encompassing the entire span of the Gate to Ma'Swamp. This mural depicted the history of The Ogrelord and the three realms. Though in the center was what caught the attention of The Ogrelord, for there was a depiction of Him strewn across a cloud, touching His finger to the finger of a Man.

The exquisite detail that Rea had gathered from Him by only seeing Him once astounded The Ogrelord. He assured Rea that this mural would live on forever, for nothing would ever ruin it. So Rea, knowing her job in the Gate to Ma'Swamp was done, entered Ma'Swamp, where her soul could rest easy.

Chapter IV: The Tales of the Realms
The Bridge to Ma'Swamp:

When the people of Aeterna Flamma learned of the afterlife, they sought a way to get there. Since Legionnaires could not die of natural causes, they knew that they must find an alternative way to reach it. No Legionnaires knew what to do, for they were not intelligent, but they knew someone who was.

The Legionnaires went deep underground, where their leader, the King Regent, resided. They asked for his counsel for three days and three nights before he would harken to them. They asked him to aide them in reaching the afterlife. He spent quite some time pondering this, and after twenty-four days, he had an answer.

He told the Legionnaires to collect every single stone they could find, and to mortar them together, forging a bridge to the realm of Ma'Swamp. No feat such as this had ever been performed before, so the Legionnaires were eager to attempt it, if it meant completing their original goal of reaching the afterlife that waited for them in Ma'Swamp. So they scoured the realm looking for stones, they took down homes and huts, they swam in pits, they emptied their rocky roads. After many years of collecting, they started working on their bridge to happiness.

When they first started shaping the start of the bridge, goblins, the mutant Legionnaires that were cast out at birth, decided to attack them. The Legionnaires won the battle between the two forces, but at great cost, they lost many of the Legionnaires who would be helping them to build the bridge. This made the amount of work that must be done nearly double. But, with envy still ruling them, the Legionnaires accepted this work so that they may be greedy in Ma'Swamp.

After the bridge had been built from the center of Aeterna Flamma to about the outer reaches of the next city to the west, the Legionnaires were met with yet another problem; the next city wanted to reach the afterlife as well, and this city did not want to share, they wanted Ma'Swamp all to themselves. This caused uproar and riots between the cities of Legionnaires. There was yet another battle, and the Legionnaires building the bridge had even fewer numbers after winning this battle. The work progressed, but even more slowly than before.

While the bridge was being created, the Tot assigned to watch Aeterna Flamma, Lennox, warned The Ogrelord of what was happening in Aeterna Flamma. Instead of worrying, The Ogrelord simply said, "If music be the food of love, then play on." With this command, Lennox flew back to Aeterna Flamma to set up a devious distraction to stop their progress.

When the Legionnaires awoke for their next day of work, they went back to the bridge, where there were huge plates covered with hundreds of freshly made waffles. All the Legionnaires attacked each other and scrambled to get the waffles before anyone else could. Greed, envy, and hatred overwhelmed the Legionnaires. They no longer wanted to work on the bridge, they only wanted the waffles.

The waffles started battles, wars, and even group murders. It was Legionnaires against Legionnaires until only a handful of them were left standing, unable to fight due to pure exhaustion. The fighting killed so many of the Legionnaires, that they could not hope to continue to build; but the Legionnaires do not feel hope, only envy, so they kept on building, city after city. Decade after decade flew by. The Legionnaires moved three feet a week working on this bridge.

The Legionnaires became such a minor threat moving at this pace that Lennox forgot about them and watched the rest of the realm over just the bridge. This gave the Legionnaires the opportunity to cover more ground and make more progress than ever before.

As they covered more and more yards with this bridge, they were noticed more by Lennox, who eventually thought that something else should be done to slow the progress even more. He went to The Ogrelord and asked what he should do next to stop the Legionnaires. The Ogrelord gave yet another executive order. Lennox was to attack the start of the bridge, preventing any more stones from being carried across it.

Lennox flew down to Aeterna Flamma once more. Stone by stone, he took the beginning of the bridge apart, hoping it would stop the stones from being carried across. Lennox then waited to see what the Legionnaires would do. Many of them paid no mind to the gap, and simply fell down through them, others tried to jump across, but to no avail. Finally, they asked the King Regent what to do. He told them to throw Legionnaires over the gap, then throw stones to them so that they may continue to build once more. Then he dismissed them to do just that.

As Lennox watched, they carried out this plan exactly, and he watched as they resumed their work with ease. He was worried that they might actually break into Ma'Swamp, so he did what he believed was necessary and killed one of the Legionnaires that was carrying stones. It was a peaceful death, but it was a murder nonetheless. The Ogrelord was outraged, for He had been watching the actions of Lennox. He punished Lennox by taking a large amount of power away from him, making him unable to influence anything directly. He would now always need to go to The Ogrelord to get anything done.

The Legionnaires had nearly reached the gate to Ma'Swamp before The Ogrelord intervened in this affair himself. He stood before them in His avatar form, a hooded man, and they attacked Him. His patience had gone, so he struck down the entire bridge, with all of the Legionnaires on it, so that they could have their wish. They were sent immediately to Ma'Swamp, only not as the living, but as the souls of Legionnaires.

They were finally happy in Ma'Swamp, even though their rainbow bridge had been destroyed and they had been killed, they were finally reunited with their brethren in a place where they could feel more than just hatred and greed, they could love and be merry. And so they did, for the rest of eternity.

The Fourth Realm:

The entities of the realms, being their own conscious beings and having their own free will, convene to discuss the matters of the realms at the time. They have made many decisions concerning their realms and the rise and fall of power in each. Far Far Away was always more progressive, always wanting to change and become better than it was. Aeterna Flamma was very traditional. It never wanted to change much, and when it had to, it did so very slowly and carefully. Ma'Swamp was the voice of reason between them, not having that many problems in itself.

There were many topics to discuss, and they argued on how to deal with nearly all of them. There was one matter, however, that they all agreed on: they needed a new realm. The realms in which they lived were becoming polluted with mutants and beings that should not exist alongside them, and only exist because of mating between Men and Legionnaires, or Fairy Tale creatures that drank too much from the All-Star fountain in either Far Far Away or Aeterna Flamma.

They discussed how to go about the change of having one more realm to help control the beings of the realms, and even discussed which beings would be moved there and which would not. They decided to consult The Ogrelord on this matter, and allowed Him to help decide who should be placed where.

The Ogrelord agreed that a fourth realm should be forged, but was not sure of how to move all of these beings without severely disrupting the current realms. He knew that these other beings caused great harm to the residents of the other realms, but He did not want to take them away from their homes.

The Ogrelord pondered this for a while, taking His attention away from the other realms, and instead focused on this one. Then He had an idea. He would make the realm out of the bits of the other realms where the beings who were to be moved resided. This included the Enchanted Forest in Far Far Away, the Lake of Fire in Aeterna Flamma, and the Lonely Castle where the dragon resided in Ma'Swamp. He picked up these places and all of the beings who lived there, and moved them out of their past realms, this forced them together into something new, something beautiful and different. The Ogrelord had created another realm, and with it, its own entity.

This entity took shape, being an amalgam of many of the beings that resided within it, and its first words were its name, Ever After. Every being that resided in Ever After was now pleased with its own appearance and loved everything around it, not having to fear anything. There was no hatred, disgust, or war in Ever After.

All beings always had the same sense of happiness as they did the day before and the day after, never feeling other emotions. This was almost to the point of feeling absolutely nothing at all. The Ogrelord did not agree with this feeling of neutrality that these beings were feeling, but let Ever After tend to its own as it so wished, whether it decided to make extreme happiness or depression.

Ever After met with the other entities the next time they convened to discuss problems in the realms. The entity harkened, not understanding what these "problems" were. "Is not all in you filled with happiness and glamour?" asked Ever After. The other entities explained to it that in order for each being in itself to have true feeling, there must be hard times, sadness, even fear, however bad it may seem. This was the only way to truly give these beings happiness in a world of perfection, there must be something there to upset the peace.

Ever After considered what its siblings had told it, and decided that they were right. There must be chaos amongst the perfection that overwhelmed itself. So Ever After created a new being, of malice and destruction. It only ever had one feeling, hatred. This being attacked whenever it felt like, but never killed. It attacked throughout the realm forever, leaving entire cities alone but in fear.

The realm was seemingly infinite, so it took many centuries before it was able to attack all over. After being attacked and filled with fear, these cities would rise up once more in happiness and rejoice that they survived the attack. Beings could finally feel again.

Ever After knew it had done the right thing, for its beings had become even happier with just a bit of chaos added in. That taught all of the entities, and even The Ogrelord that some chaos was needed in order to have great happiness throughout the realms.

From then on, the fourth realm became a place of happiness for all of the beings that resided there, despite the immortal hunter, The Big Bad Wolf. The other beings feared it rightly so, but when it was gone, they had many celebrations and their worship in The Ogrelord grew even stronger.

The Gambles of Rumpelstiltskin:

After the death of the first great king of Far Far Away, the kingdom fell under hard times. In this, there were many Men who started to deceive, steal, and commit other crimes against one another. Crime became more rampant, and people were unkind to one another over all. There was one Man who many saw as a helper, but they did not know his true self, or even his true name.

This Man made pacts with others, who gambled away what they loved without knowing what it really meant to them. He did this all in secret, knowing that nobody could follow him without his name. He used his name against the people, telling them that if they could guess it, their contracts would be considered undone.

He was treacherous to those he made deals with, offering them exactly what their hearts desired, but at a terrible cost, often an unborn child, a home, once even an entire kingdom. Though after years of these gambles, with many people having sacrificed their homes, loved ones, and riches, one young woman but an end to his reign of power by finding him chanting his true name in the forest, the name Rumpelstiltskin.

After being shamed for the pacts he had made, he simply said, "And what's he then that says I'm the villain? When this advice is free I give, and honest?"

This was a compelling argument, for sure. It was good enough for the Men who had caught Rumpelstiltskin. They let him free, but told everyone who would listen of the consequences of gambling with him. They began to teach others about the dangers and the sad outcomes of gambling, and to never gamble more than you can afford to lose. Some men took this to heart. Others thought nothing of it, and still gambled away whatever they had to get what they wanted. They did not truly cherish what they had to begin with.

After many more years, and after losing his identity to nearly everyone in the realm, still no one seemed to give a damn about his bad reputation. People continued to go to Rumpelstiltskin to get what they wanted from him, and they still gambled away the things they loved. No man or woman that was consumed by greed ever gave a second thought to the arrangement until they realized the great losses they had suffered, but by then, it was too late.

Rumpelstiltskin never quite rose to the power he once had. However, he had made enough deals to sit on a throne of lies for the rest of his days. As for the people who gambled and lost, The Ogrelord saw to it that they were well taken care of in Ma'Swamp, and the errors of their ways explained to them. The Ogrelord sent word down to His priests telling them to preach of the dangers of gambling, and to tell people only to gamble in moderation, never while in times of trouble risking what you already have.

The Thirteenth King Regent:

All of the Legionnaires in Aeterna Flamma were present during the birth of the Thirteenth King Regent, their soon-to-be King. As the infant matured into boy, they found that he was different than most other boys, and was not social like the twelve King Regents before him. His father said that it was due to his rather unusual upbringing, having no mother. Most people accepted that as a fact, knowing that only a lack of motherly love could make a boy so cold hearted.

This boy committed many cruel and violent acts throughout his childhood. He would throw rocks at passing animals. He would cause other children to cry with his harsh words. He even had a Legionnaire put to death for nothing more than giving him too much sugar in his tea.

Each of these acts was told to be the result of a motherless upbringing, but that is not the truth. True, the boy had no mother, but that was no excuse for the tortuous manner with which he treated others around him. Over time, many grew to fear this King Regent, including his father. The boy did not seem to care. He always had the same look about him, as if he were truly dead inside, unable to feel any emotion.

After years had passed, the boy's father died under mysterious circumstances, allowing for the boy to become the new King Regent. This King Regent was unlike any other. At the slightest hint of defiance, he had many innocents publicly executed in the streets to show that he would have no mercy. This King Regent went to war over thirty times during his reign, and destroyed his own people without a second thought. More than six million Legionnaires were slaughtered needlessly. It came to the attention of Lennox quite often, and Lennox told The Ogrelord of what was happening. However, The Ogrelord did not interfere, for fear of taking away the free will of his subjects. With a heavy heart, The Ogrelord allowed this reign to continue.

The King Regent never showed any emotion. He never displayed hatred, nor fear, nor even love for his bride and child. He ruled using this emotional neutrality to strike fear into his subjects. It then came to the attention of Lennox that this King Regent was different for one very peculiar reason. This King Regent was the only being in existence without any layer. This is why he was empty emotionally.

He never showed any love, fear, or hatred because those emotions were not a part of him. How this could happen, Lennox did not know. Neither did The Ogrelord. They just allowed the King Regent to continue his reign as an empty being, eventually dying alone, but not sad. He felt nothing when his wife died and his son ended his rule in a similar fashion to how this King Regent ended his father's.

This King Regent was not the only being to have no layer. There were many more. All irregularities in the realms, and were not to be trifled with, for they would feel nothing when they ended you. The Ogrelord did nothing to any of these irregularities, claiming that these beings were an extremely complex matter that should not be changed. He understood that they willed themselves into existence rather than being f into existence. They were beings of pure will, and The Ogrelord could not interfere with the wills of beings in the realms.

Many horrors were committed by these irregularities, but The Ogrelord stopped none. The only escape from these beings was to try and give them as much of the love layer as possible so as to try and show them emotion. The Ogrelord could give away no layer to these beings, and instead asked that the priests of His religion show as much love and kindness as possible to all, so that those irregularities would be shown the emotional layers.

Layer 73

Jon and the Dragon:

Long ago, there was one man who was born with an extra layer, the layer of defiance. This layer was more prominent that the rest, and so he defied all, and was outcast from society. The Ogrelord watched this man, who was given the name Jon with pity. The Ogrelord had never intended any beings to have such a powerful and prominent layer. The layer was so powerful that the man had no place to exist, for he was defiant in all areas. Because he was not able to live anywhere due to his immense power of defiance, he wandered. Jon wandered to the Far East. Upon his arrival at the edge of the world, he was greeted by The Ogrelord. Staring out into the gap between the realms, and seeing the small, brilliantly lit lights illuminating it, Jon watched as they moved, one by one. As they moved, they came closer together until they eventually formed a mosaic in the embodiment of The Ogrelord.

The Ogrelord spoke to Jon, and Jon listened intently, hoping The Ogrelord could guide him in the right direction. The Ogrelord said, "Love is merely a madness." It was then that Jon realized that his whole life had been lived by a code of defiance. He knew that he must overcome it with the quest that The Ogrelord gave him, to reach the fair city of Worcestershire.

As the image of The Ogrelord faded, He left Jon with one more piece of knowledge; the existence of Jon's layer of defiance.

Jon carried this burden with him, as he tried desperately to reach Worcestershire, but to no avail. For many years, Jon tried, but whenever he was ordered to do something, he did the opposite. This made the struggle much greater for Jon, so Jon did what must be done, he set out alone. Jon ventured out to the east of Far Far Away, making sure he only had contact with himself. But even this proved to be a challenge, for he was not able to travel easily alone, and only during the day, due to the many evils of the dark. Wandering alone on afternoon, Jon met a man named Ben. Feeling lonely after all of his travel, Jon asked Ben to accompany him for a short while. The two men spoke for a long time during the journey, and became quite close.

Finally, Jon told Ben about his curse. Ben took this to heart, and was extra careful to not give orders to Jon. This worked until they had reached the outskirts of Worcestershire. Ben accidentally told Jon, "Go on, enter Worcestershire, my friend." Jon was immediately doomed to leave then, and take not one look back.

Jon ventured for months, wandering aimlessly on and on. He laid one night, looking up at the sky as the sun retired when he saw a bright flash of crimson in the sky. He thought nothing of it and drifted into sleep as twilight fell.

When Jon awoke, he was in the very belly of the beast he witnessed the night before, the dragon. Jon was terrified, for he did not want to die. Being willful, Jon kept alive off of the food he found crushed up inside of the dragon. Days turned to weeks. When Jon finally made his way out of the dragon, he knew not where he was. He wandered. The bright light blinding him as he stumbled around. Jon found a man, a man hooded in a swamp-green robe. Jon asked the man where he was, and with pride in his voice, the man removed His hood to reveal the starry avatar of The Ogrelord Jon had witnessed before. The Ogrelord said unto him, "Worcestershire." And as The Ogrelord cured him Jon said, "Ooh, spicy."

The Blanket of Seasons:

In the days of the Realms' youth, many people tilled the dirt hoping to farm many foods to sustain life. They found that it was nearly impossible, due to the cold temperatures that were always there. Try as they may, many crops would die whilst trying to grow. The farmers of the time prayed to their gods, and many prayed to The Ogrelord. They asked Him to help their crops grow to fruition. He had to think of a way to resolve this issue before He could solve it.

He watched the way that His creations stayed warm, and noticed that some sat and slept by fires. The Ogrelord took the purest fire from the realm of Ma'Swamp, and placed it below the grounds in the realm, deep enough to warm the dirt.

For a while this worked, heating up all of the realms' ground. But as time passed, the blaze grew and spread under the realms' dirt and made the world hotter and hotter, causing the roots of crops to catch fire, and the crops to die. Farmers did not realize the true cause of this until the ground beneath them became so hot it would dry up the soil. The ground grew ever hotter, and was eventually so hot it would burn the feet of the people who walked upon it.

The Ogrelord saw this problem and had to work quickly to fix it. He sent Lodovico to gather his brethren and together they were to weep onto the realms. As they wept, the ground soaked up the water, dousing the fires enough that the dirt and soil were able to be walked upon. The internal fire was still awesome and powerful. Now that the internal fire was not such a powerful force, The Ogrelord took a great shell and within it He placed this great fire, leaving the shell and all its contents deep below the dirt and soil of the realms, to be a minor source of heat.

With no other ideas on how to heat the world, He once again began watching his realms for inspiration. He watched many of them, one at a time, until He saw a mother wrap up her infantile child in a blanket she had sewn.

This gave The Ogrelord a new idea. He would coat the realms in a blanket of warmth, made from the fur on His back. He spent six long months weaving this blanket for the realms. After these six months, The Ogrelord took this blanket and spread it over Ma'Swamp. He then went to where Aeterna Flamma was located and covered that. Then, upon reaching Far Far Away, the blanket ran out. The Ogrelord decided then that every six months, He would shift the blanket from Ma'Swamp to Far Far Away, and from Far Far Away to Ma'Swamp.

He gave this cloth the name, "The Blanket of Seasons," and told His priests to explain this to their fellow beings. The priests did so, and soon every follower of The Ogrelord knew of the Blanket of Seasons, of the seasons that the realms would now have, and of the new layer that the realms had.

Chapter V: The End
The Ogrelord's Final Stand:

After waiting for many decades in his home of Aeterna Flamma, The King Regent had amassed an army of Legionnaires that he believed was sizeable enough for him to take over all of the realms. He rose from his pit in Aeterna Flamma and moved his army to The Enchanted Forest, attacking all of those who would resist him and his army. Waves of Legionnaires moved throughout the forest, forcing them out of their homes and into the land of Ma'Swamp.

The Ogrelord took notice of the attacks on this land, and rose up to defend the people of the Enchanted Forest. The Ogrelord appeared in solid form for the first time since before the creation of the worlds. The world itself seemed to warp into the center of The Ogrelord as he took form in the Enchanted Forest.

With heavy heart, and his layer of hatred for war becoming prominent, The Ogrelord eliminated the Legionnaires that were attacking the Enchanted Forest. They were delivered directly into Ma'Swamp. Within seconds, the invasion was put to an end.

The Ogrelord's true form was then revealed to the Men, creatures, and Legionnaires, and all understood. They understood who He was, and why He created the realms, but they could not explain it. It was a knowledge that they knew, but could not explain.

They all stood there, looking up at His magnificence and His gargantuan solid form. The Men, mostly, were the ones impacted by this. The Legionnaires were not so impacted, and used this as a chance to attack.

The Ogrelord took the Men and the Fairy Tale creatures and moved them into Far Far Away for their safety. He then gave the attacking Legionnaires forgiveness before sending the rest of their army to Ma'Swamp for all eternity. When He looked around, there was no more army in the Enchanted Forest. The Ogrelord's solid form moved to Ma'Swamp. There, on the wall, The King Regent and his army was waiting.

The Ogrelord met with The King Regent, who had a form nearly equal in size to The Ogrelord. The King Regent spoke to the remainder of his army, whom he had taken with him to the wall of Ma'Swamp. He told them that this new land was theirs, and nothing could stop them, not even The Ogrelord.

The army was riled up and ready for this invasion. In plain view of The Ogrelord, who was watching to see what would happen, the King Regent kicked a hole in the wall of Ma'Swamp, letting his Legionnaires in to wreak havoc.

The Ogrelord, in magnificent purity, and His layer of hatred for war still showing, yelled, "What are you doing in Ma'Swamp?"

After He yelled this, the King Regent threatened to destroy the entirety of Ma'Swamp, leaving nothing but ruin and corpses. The Ogrelord said to the King Regent who threatened His realm, "Oh, really? You and what army?"

When the King Regent turned around, his army had been torn apart by fairy tale creatures and the rest were cheering on The Ogrelord in this battle.

The Ogrelord battled the King Regent with great speed and unmatched power. The Ogrelord's five layers all became one, allowing Him to feel a range of new emotions. This had never happened to Him before, and He was shocked. In His shock and confusion, the King Regent mortally wounded The Ogrelord.

All of the people in all of the realms were in shock, including the Legionnaires. They stopped their attack on the realm of Ma'Swamp, coming to be with The Ogrelord in His final moments. The Ogrelord looked around at His realm, shedding a single tear that was then collected in a bottle.

The Ogrelord knew what he had to do. He looked to His most devoted worshippers, three creatures from the Enchanted Forest and two Men from Far Far Away, and He ascended them to godhood. He set them in place so that they could rule where He was no longer able to be.

The Ogrelord fell to the ground, on His back, slowly fading away into the Void. He smiled, and He said His final words before His layer was given to the new Gods he had made. Each having a layer that once belonged to Him, The Ogrelord spoke, "When I saw you I fell in love, and you smiled because you knew."

The Ogrelord forgave the King Regent as He faded, allowing the King Regent to pass on into the afterlife without any hatred in his heart. The King Regent died, finally experiencing the layer of The Ogrelord, and he died happy.

The new Gods sealed off Ma'Swamp and delivered the Legionnaires back to Aeterna Flamma, where they went back to life as usual. Their lives moved on, and over time, they forgot about this encounter. All of the beings affected by their encounter with The Ogrelord eventually lost all memory of their encounter with Him.

Though all of those beings lost their memories, they retained the goodness He had left in them. Throughout all of the realms, everyone eventually lost all knowledge of other realms and of The Ogrelord, only a few people still worshipping Him. This became the legacy of The Ogrelord, and His church took notice and recorded it.

The new Gods that were appointed took over the mantle of The Ogrelord, guiding the realms as He would. The land of Ma'Swamp went back to perfect harmony. The layer of The Ogrelord was at peace.

The New Gods and Their Layer:

The first of the new Gods is Queen L, a woman from Far Far Away, where she once ruled. She took on the Outer Layer of The Ogrelord. She expresses incredible and undying love for Men and the people in the realms.

The second new God is Little Kitty, a creature from the Enchanted Forest blessed with the Second Layer, the red layer of hatred for war. He hates all things when he lets the layer show.

The third new God is the Ginger-Bread Man, a creature that lived in the Enchanted Forest. He was granted the Third Layer, the blue layer of creativity. His skin goes an even deeper blue when his layer is fully prominent.

The fourth new God is The Big Bad Wolf, the last creature to have ascended to Godhood. He was given the Fourth Layer of blinding white intelligence. When this layer is fully active and showing, nobody can be near him, for it means he is thinking and his light is too bright.

The last of the new Gods is King H, Queen L's husband. King H was given the Fifth Layer of sadness and it is a depressing blue. When this layer is fully shown, King H must go off to look into the Void and ponder life, much like The Ogrelord did.

These new Gods are in complete control of the realms, and will defend it until the End of All Things, when all things must die.

The End of All Things:

This is a prophecy of events to come, and it will signify the end of all things. The new anti-Gods don't do much on their own, but they will counter the actions of the Gods in control of the realms. These anti-Gods will bring about the end of all things. They will prevent any more lessons from being taught about The Ogrelord.

The first signal of the end is the containment of every Fairy Tale creature, this will come about when the Legionnaires do it in honor of their anti-Gods. The containment of these creatures will keep them from the coming battle.

The second signal of the end is the elimination of the swamps in the realms. They will all dry up and turned into fields. This will come about when the anti-Gods decide to undo the work of The Ogrelord Himself.

The final signal of the end is the destruction of the onions. This will come about when the anti-Gods take the symbol as a personal offense to themselves and destroy each one.

The events of the End will go as follows, our five new Gods will enter a glorious battle with the anti-Gods of the Legionnaires. This battle will be the death of all of them, and the destruction of all of their layer combined. This battle will be reflected throughout every realm and its power will be so mighty that the entirety of the Void will be illuminated by layer. When the Void is lit by layer, it will be the absolute mark of the end. The five new God will die in battle against the anti-Gods, who will also die in the battle.

The Void will sweep over the realms, destroying all in its path, leaving only the bare land of each realm. All Men, Legionnaires, and creatures will perish. Only Ma'swamp will stand above, nearly untouched by the awful destruction. After the Void is finished, and returns to its serene stillness, the caretakers of Ma'Swamp will take the tear that The Ogrelord shed on His deathbed and they will use it to bring back life to each realm, starting over from the beginning.

At the end of it all, The Ogrelord will come back from Void to rule the new realms. The world will start over and repeat the process for all Eternity.

Jacob Emmons began writing this story while still a sophomore in high school. What started as a joke among friends soon became the inspiration for an entire religion based around one of his favorite fictional characters.

Jacob is now a freshman in college and is pursuing a career in Literature.

Made in the USA
Middletown, DE
17 October 2016